THE
Christmas Secret

(José's Christmas Secret)

by JOAN LEXAU

Pictures by DON BOLOGNESE

SCHOLASTIC INC.

New York   Toronto   London   Auckland   Sydney

pro Matička s láska

ISBN 0-590-40615-9

Copyright © 1963 by Joan M. Lexau.

All rights reserved. Published by Scholastic Inc.,
730 Broadway, New York, NY 10003, by arrangement with
Dial Books for Young Readers, a division of E. P. Dutton,
Inc. LUCKY STAR is a trademark of Scholastic Inc.

12 11 10 9 8 7 6 5 4 3   8 9/8 0 1/9

Printed in the U.S.A.   28

José was ten years old, and the man of the family. He could not get to sleep. There was too much to think about.

"José, what is it?" his mother asked. "Are you too cold to sleep?"

"No, Mami," José said. "I am not the one who is cold. Why don't you take one of our warm blankets? Tomás and I have each other to keep us warm." Tomás, his seven-year-old brother, slept with him on the mattress on the floor.

Every night José begged his mother to take one of the two wool blankets. Hers were only cotton. Every night she said, "No, José. You have to sleep on the floor where the cold air goes. I will be all right. Do not worry."

But how could he help but worry? His father had died of pneumonia last spring, only a month after they left Puerto Rico. Ever since then his mother had looked so afraid and alone.

José remembered, with a sick feeling in his stomach, how it was after the funeral. The money they had brought from Puerto Rico was almost gone. They had thought it would last so long.

In Puerto Rico, the neighbors — no matter how poor — would have helped them. But, as Mami said, this was a cold land. In New York, even the neighbors were strangers.

His mother said once, "On the island you have so little it does not matter if you share it. You come here, to the mainland, to do better and you work so hard for it. But always you are afraid things will go back to the way they were before."

Mrs. Rodriguez, a woman in their building, helped them. Her parents had come from the island but she could not speak much Spanish herself.

The day after the funeral she came to their door and said shyly, "They need someone at the hotel and I thought you might be wanting a job. The boss said to bring you tomorrow. They'll train you and you don't need much English."

So Mami went to work at the hotel. They had talked the landlord into waiting a few more weeks for the rent. José and Tomás taught Mami English as they learned more new words at school.

They were able to eat. Yet they were always a little hungry.

They had clothes, but not many. Their mother had a coat that had been warm in the spring but was not meant for December.

And they had a home. Their apartment was on the top floor and rain leaked through the roof in summer. But beds could be moved out of the way.

There was no way to get away from the winter cold.

José listened to the wind forcing its way around the newspapers Mami put over the windows. The wind even came through the walls where the plaster was gone.

Home should be a place to be warm, José thought.

"It is up to me to get Mami a blanket," he said to himself. "Christmas is coming in six more days. God, let me get Mami a blanket for Christmas."

José fell asleep trying to think of ways to earn the money for a blanket. The next morning he thought about it as he folded the mattress and dragged it to a corner, out of the way.

José and Tomás did the dishes while their mother packed her lunch.

"I will do that," she said. "You will have enough dishwashing when you go to be soldiers."

"No, Mami. This is good exercise for us," José said.

Tomás rubbed a dish so hard he almost dropped it.

"Children should not talk back to their elders," their mother said.

Tomás and José grinned.

Mami laughed as she lightly tapped them each on the ear. "And now I must go. Be good at the school, you two, and come right home."

"Yes, Mami," Tomás promised. José said nothing. An idea was coming and he was not sure he could come right home. His mother hurried out so she would not be late for work.

José was still thinking about his idea in school while the teacher talked.

"José, tell me about Columbus," he heard Mrs. Adams say.

"In 1493 he came to Puerto Rico," José said quickly.

The class laughed and even the teacher smiled.

"We were talking about state capitals," Mrs. Adams said.

"I am sorry," said José. But he went on thinking his own thoughts. He couldn't stop.

He thought about it later while they

worked on the cardboard boxes they were making for their mothers. José painted his red and white for the hot sun shining on a sandy beach.

"This is good," José thought. "So is the calendar Tomás is making with a picture of flowers pasted on it. But Mami shall have a much finer present."

By the time school was out, José knew what he had to do. He had to find a job in the neighborhood. And he had to be home by six when Mami came home.

But what about Tomás? Everything Tomás knew came pouring out of his mouth. José did not like to have secrets from Mami but if she knew, she would say, "You are too little to worry so much." She would not let him get a job, and there would be no blanket.

As they left the school, José said, "Tomás, can you keep a secret?"

"Sure," Tomás said. "Anyway, who would I tell?"

"I mean from Mami," said José.

"Don't worry," Tomás said. "I won't tell her about the box you are making."

"It is not the box," José said. "And you told her about what you are making. Who knows what you will tell next?"

"It's my own present," said Tomás. "I can tell her about my own present. Tell me the secret. I won't tell her."

"Well, I will tell you part of it," José said as they reached their building. "I am not coming up with you. I will be home when Mami comes. If you keep that part, I will tell you the rest tomorrow. It is a good secret, one she will like if she does not know of it too soon."

Tomás stared at his brother. They were *niños de casa,* children of the home. They could go only to and from school without their mother. All kinds of bad things could happen in the city, she said. The only way to stay out of trouble was to stay away from it. But in warm weather it was hard to watch the other children playing. And to make it worse, the children made fun of them. Often the brothers had argued with their mother about this. They had even played outside a few times — but always together.

"I will go with you," Tomás said. "I will help you."

"You can help by not asking questions. Go on in now." José took the key from around his neck and gave it to Tomás.

Tomás made a face but he went into the building without another word.

José asked at the bakery and the Chinese laundry but they had no job. At the supermarket, José said, "I will sweep or anything." No, he was too little.

Everywhere it was, "No, niño, no job."
He saw a man selling Christmas trees.
"Do you have a job for me?" said José.
"I'm sorry, son," the man said. "Business
is bad. Too many people selling trees and
too few with money to buy them."

"Oh," said José. "Well, thank you anyway." He turned away slowly. He had been so sure he could get a job somehow.

"Wait a minute," said the man. "Tell you what. If you want to try, I'll give you a dime for each tree you sell."

José wanted to shout, to sing! But he kept the shouting inside.

"I will sell them," he told the man.

José picked up a little tree and stood in the middle of the sidewalk. "Very special trees. Very cheap," he said.

A few people smiled but no one stopped.

"See what I mean?" said the man.

José kept trying until Mr. Sands told him it was nearly six. After asking if he could come back tomorrow, he ran home.

Tomás had set up the dominoes on the table as though two were playing. "That was a good idea," José said as he sat down and picked up a domino.

That night Tomás did not tell the secret, and the more he did not tell it, the more he thought about it. He could hardly look at his mother.

After dinner as she sewed a button on his coat, she said, "You are sick or you have done something bad. Which is it?"

Tomás looked at José, but José could not help him.

Mami said, "There is nothing so bad you cannot tell me. Are you afraid I will punish you? But what of that? After the punishing, it is all over and we will never speak of it again. It will be like it never was. Now tell me."

Tomás stared at the needle going in

and out. At last he said, "I am sorry the button came off my coat, Mami."

"That is not it," said his mother. "Buttons go on and off. It is no matter. Now tell me."

Tomás looked away from his mother and said, "I wish I didn't tell you about the calendar. It is not a surprise now."

His mother laughed. "Is that all? I have already forgotten what you told me about it. Anyway, I have not seen the picture, and that is the important part. Do not worry me like that."

José let out a sigh. All right so far.

The next day at school José figured out how many trees he had to sell.

"Five dollars should buy a warm blanket," he thought.

He had to multiply ten cents many times before he found that fifty of them would make five dollars. Fifty trees.

"José, what are you doing?" asked his teacher.

"Multiplying," said José.

"We did that an hour ago," she said.

"I am sorry," he said.

After school he told Tomás about the blanket. "Someday," he went on, "I will get Mami a fine apartment with an elevator instead of all those stairs, and a warm coat, and a new tooth for the one in front that is gone. And I will take her back to the island."

Tomás said angrily, "Yes, you will do all that and what can I do?"

José stood in front of his brother. "Could I do all these things alone?" he asked. "Could I get the blanket if you didn't keep it a secret? It will be from both of us. I will tell Mami so."

"I could help you sell trees. Or I could get a job of my own," said Tomás.

"No," José said. "Now one of us is minding Mami and that is a good thing."

"O.K.," said Tomás. "But you don't have to take me home every day. I'm big enough to go alone."

Tomás went on ahead. But soon he stopped and waited for José. "I don't like to walk by myself. There is no one to talk to," he said.

"Then we will just walk together after this," José said.

He left his brother at the apartment and ran to the Christmas tree stand. He took his little tree and called out, "Very special trees. Very cheap."

Some people scowled at him as he stood in their way, but by 5:45 he sold two trees. He delivered one and the lady gave him a quarter. Mr. Sands said he could keep what he made delivering trees.

"Can you hold the money for me for a while?" asked José. He didn't know where he could hide it at home.

"Sure," Mr. Sands said. "Just say the word when you want it."

José hurried home. Tomás opened the door before he could knock.

"Forty-five cents," José said. "Not much, but a start." Three more days to go.

The next afternoon the first person who came by the stand was Mrs. Rodriguez. He tried to hide his face behind the tree he was holding but it was too late.

"José, does your mother know you aren't home?" Mrs. Rodriguez asked.

José said, "I have never seen you come home this early. I hope you are not ill."

Mrs. Rodriguez laughed. "Don't change the subject. I had some time off coming. José, you know I won't tell your mother what's going on if I don't have to."

There was no choice, so José told her about the blanket. "If you tell her," he said, "she will make me stop."

"Every Christmas I wish I had a tree to cheer me up. I'll be with you people Christmas day but still I'd like to have one. If I buy it from you, I won't dare tell your secret," she said.

José gladly sold her a tree and said he would deliver it on his way home. After that he sold six little trees and a great big one. Mr. Sands gave him twenty cents for selling the big tree. He made fifteen cents delivering one tree and a quarter for another, but he took no money from

Mrs. Rodriguez. His mother would be angry if he did that.

A dollar and seventy-five cents, and two more days.

That evening Tomás found the secret heavy. Was it right for him to know something Mami could not be told? He could not eat or speak.

At the end of supper Mami said, "Stay where you are, you two. Tomás, for days you have been acting strange, and tonight strangest of all. What is it?"

Tomás looked away and said nothing.

Mami put her hands on his shoulders. "See, here we are, just the two of us, and it is time for the truth. Was it the truth you told me the other day when I asked you what was wrong?"

"It was the truth, but not that truth," Tomás whispered. He buried his face in his mother's lap and howled, "Don't make me tell. It's not my secret."

Mami ran her fingers gently through his hair and looked at José.

There was a long silence. Tomás sat up and also stared at his brother.

José thought a bit and then said, "Mami, I am not the boss of this family. But I am the man of the family, and there are things I have to do."

"But to have a secret from me, José? This you must do?" asked his mother.

José said, "The secret is not something I am doing for me."

"For me, José?" his mother asked.

"Yes, Mami. And if you say I must tell, I will. But I hope you will not."

His mother rubbed her forehead as if she could rub all the worry away. "Without a father in the family it is hard to know what to do. And living in a foreign country, everything is so strange —"

"But it is not a foreign country. It is ours, as much as the island. We are citizens, all of us," José said.

"Yes, I come here a citizen and have to learn to speak all over again," Mami said angrily. "And we must live by the clock as if we are machines. Remember when you were to go to the zoo? You were just a little late and they went without you."

Mami took a breath and went on, "And people say we only come here to get on the welfare and let the city take care of us. Your father dreamed so long of coming here where there are more schools and more places to work. All he wanted was to work hard and make a good life for his sons. We will stay because he wanted it so. Anyway," she said, almost in tears, "there is no money to go home."

José and Tomás were silent. José knew his mother missed the island, but he had not known she felt this bad about it.

After a while Mami said lightly, "Such a way to talk so soon before Christmas. I should be thinking of the good things, not the bad. Now for your secret. One thing I know, my boys are good boys. If

I did not know this — Well, anyway, you may have your secret."

"You will not be sorry," José said. He went to bed with a lighter heart but still he was not sure of the blanket.

The next day he sold four trees and made twenty cents for delivering one. Two dollars and thirty-five cents.

Mami said nothing about the secret. After they ate their rice and beans, they took out the box with the Christmas scene. On top of the dresser they put Mary, Joseph, the Infant, and the donkey. The Three Kings were put on the windowsill. Each day they would be moved closer until Three Kings Day. When they all agreed it was just right, they stood back to admire their work.

It made Christmas seem very near. Already José could almost taste the roast pork. It would not be the same as a whole roast pig cooked outdoors, but still he could hardly wait. And they would have *arroz con dulce*, something like a rice pudding with cinnamon in it.

But if he could, he would have pushed Christmas ahead to give him more time.

José prayed very hard that night. "God, you know tomorrow is Christmas Eve and I am not even halfway to a blanket. I do not have to go to school tomorrow, but something has to happen before Mami comes home at one. Amen."

He added, *"Por favor* — please!" Maybe two languages would help.

After their mother left the next morning, José said, "I want you to pray hard, Tomás, harder than you ever have. Only that way will a blanket come."

"I will," promised Tomás.

"Good," José said, and he ran out.

Mr. Sands had four trees for him to deliver and that gave him eighty cents.

For two hours José stood in the cold and sold three trees. Not many people went by.

"Can I take a tree down to 125th Street?" José asked.

"Why not? Good luck," Mr. Sands said.

José ran. As soon as he sold this tree, he would be back for another.

He reached 125th Street and walked to a very busy place and shouted, "Very special trees. Very cheap. Last day."

But everyone was hurrying, hurrying. The people looked ahead in sad or angry stares, as they always did.

José stood for an hour, stamping his feet to get warm. This was the coldest day he had ever known. On the island he heard about the cold in New York but he had not understood it could be this bad.

It began to snow, slowly and then harder. The snow stabbed at his cheeks. His feet and hands were prickly from the cold.

A clock in a store window showed that it was noon. José was trying so hard not to cry. His mother always said, "When you feel like crying, sing — sing the tears away." Maybe that was why she often sang to them at night.

José closed his eyes and sang in Spanish about Puerto Rico as a land where flowers and fruits are always growing. This only made him colder.

"Not for anything would I change this land where I had the good fortune to be born!" he sang. But he was not there, he was here, and the song did not help.

Very quietly he began a happy song they had learned at school:

"Oh, Christmas tree, oh, Christmas tree..." and then louder and louder as he felt the tears coming.

"HOW LOVELY ARE YOUR BRANCHES..."

When the song was over, he felt tears sting his cheeks. He opened his eyes and saw a crowd around him. José looked at the tree. Its branches were covered with snow, adding a new beauty.

A woman asked him why he was standing there singing and holding a Christmas tree.

"Very special trees. Very cheap. Last day," José said, his voice shaking.

"I'll take it," three people said.

"Is this your last tree?" a man asked.

"Oh, no," José said. "Just a short way from here I have many fine trees. I will show you." He started walking, praying they would follow. Many did.

"You sing with me," José said shyly. The people laughed and joined in:

"Oh, come, all ye faithful . . ."

Others stared, asked questions, and followed as if they could not help it.

"What's this, a parade?" a policeman asked and then followed along.

José sold many trees. "Tomás must be praying very hard," he thought.

"Merry Christmas, Merry Christmas!" everyone called as they left.

José counted the money Mr. Sands gave

him. Four dollars and fifty-five cents. Not what he wanted, but maybe enough.

"Thank you very much," said José.

"Thank *you*. And here's a bonus," Mr. Sands said, pulling out a big tree.

José started to thank him again but Mr. Sands said, "You earned it, José. Now tell me. What do you need the money for so badly? Maybe I can help. You've helped me a lot."

José told him about the blanket. "With this money, maybe I can buy one."

"Hmm," said Mr. Sands. "That's not much. I could add a little to it."

José shook his head. "I have earned this and I will see what it can buy."

"Well, I'll tell you how I might help. My brother-in-law has a store on 125th. He said he wished his kids had half your get-up-and-go. I know he'd give you a good price on a blanket. Here, I'll give you a note for him." Mr. Sands told him how to get to the store.

José was too excited to think of taking the tree home first. By the time he reached the store, his shoulders ached, but he didn't care.

He soon found Mr. Andrews and gave him the note.

"Glad to meet you, José," he said. "Let's go to the blanket counter."

"Color?" Mr. Andrews asked.

"Red," José said quickly.

"Something very nice in red," Mr. Andrews said to a saleswoman.

José had his blanket. He tried to thank Mr. Andrews.

"*Por nada*," Mr. Andrews said. "You see — I know that means 'for nothing.' Good luck, José, and Merry Christmas."

"Same to you," said José.

José dragged the tree with one arm and held the blanket box in the other. At his building he stopped to catch his breath and then called, "Tomás, help me."

It was Mami who came to the window. José had forgotten the time. "José! What have you done!" she screamed. In a moment she and Tomás were downstairs.

His mother took the tree and Tomás took the box. On the way up, Mami said quickly in Spanish, "I get home and my boys are not here so I run out. There is Tomás coming home and I am about to hit him although I never hit my boys in the street. But he says he was in the church praying so how can I hit him for that? And he will not say where his brother is. But what I must know is, have you been stealing, José? How else could

you get this tree and what is in the box —
answer me that..."

As soon as they were in their room, José
took the box, tore it open, and let the
blanket spill out to the floor.

"*Madre de Dios!*" his mother prayed.

José told his mother all that had
happened.

But she just looked at him. He had to tell her three times before she understood.

Then she put the blanket on the bed and they all admired it. "Oh, my son, what can I say?" she said, hugging him.

"It is nothing," said José. "And it is from Tomás, too — from both of us."

"I was so worried it would be a sad

Christmas. I could buy so little," Mami said. "But now you have done this wonderful thing. Oh, your father would be so proud of his sons!"

They put the tree in a bucket of water and leaned it against the wall.

"See how the whole room is brighter," Mami said. "Later we will stand by it and sing all the songs *de Navidad* we know."

"Tomorrow you can open the presents we made at school," said Tomás.

"There just might be something for my two fine sons," their mother said.

That evening, in the middle of a song, she stopped singing. "I have just had a thought. Is it a good thing for the man of the family to be a *niño de casa?*"

José and Tomás laughed.

"But you must promise to always stay together when I am not here," Mami said.

The brothers promised.

"Very good," Mami said. "You are no longer *niños de casa*. When it is not too

cold you may play outside until I come home."

That night José whispered to his mother, "Are you asleep?"

"I am too happy for that," she said.

"Is it such a cold land still?"

"Are you telling your mother what to think now? You are indeed a bad boy."

"Sí, Mami," said José.

"Well, then, go to sleep."

"*Buenas noches*, Mami."

"*Buenas noches*, my son."

There was no shivering that night. It was as if they were lying on the white sands of the beach with the sun overhead.